Koi Girls

By Cathy Sosnowski

ISBN: 1492825999
ISBN 13: 9781492825999

For my mother, Rose Marie Sears, who was the first to put a book into my hands and set me on a lifelong path of wonder and delight.

My deepest thanks go to my husband, Jerry, who implored me to write for decades and to Ralph Marino, Kathy Polansky, Barbara Wood and all my Gentle Readers for their unwavering support.

I am particularly grateful to my first professional editor, David St. Albans, who helped me to "follow my bliss" and to believe this dream could really come true!

And last but not least, I thank the students of St. Mary of Mount Carmel School who taught me in the sweetest possible way that sharing a dream is a wonderful thing! I love you all!

Cathy Sosnowski

TABLE OF CONTENTS

CHAPTER ONE
Taking It to Heart

Justine trudged along the walking trail that followed a small stream near her new hometown. The trees were newly green, the air fresh. The sky was blue, and the stream gurgled quietly.

She sighed deeply, trying to lose the unhappy feelings that were just *ruining* a perfect spring day.

Three weeks ago, she and her family had come to this sleepy little town on the promise of a good job for her dad and a nice place for all three of them to live. Her Aunt Trish and Uncle Max lived here, and they helped her family settle into the cute house on a tree-lined street that looked like something out of a movie or an old TV show.

Everything should have been perfect...except it wasn't.

Fresh tears formed in her big blue eyes and since there wasn't anyone around, she didn't care when they slid down her face and dripped off her pointy chin.

"Dog Bone…can you imagine *that*…" she thought with an ache in her heart. The Cool Girls (they actually called themselves that!) had been laughing at her behind her back and had given her the nickname because she was so skinny and had such white skin. A couple of boys who hung around the Cool Girls had barked at her, making them laugh and Justine turn as red as her hair.

Three weeks of being teased had left her dreading each day and ready to flee the school as fast as she could. She tried to stay out of sight and take the long way home so that she would have a chance to let the bad feelings ease up, find a smile, stick it on her face, and walk into her house, pretending everything was fine—just fine.

"Why did they have to pick on me?" she complained to herself. She had never bothered anybody and had always tried to get along with everybody. They had everything Cool Girls could want: beautiful hair, perfect bodies, pretty faces, great teeth, and lots of money (guessing from the clothes they wore). They were smart. They were popular. They were the officers in every club.

"Why waste time pestering someone like *me*?" Justine wondered. She hated her hair, which was fiery red. Her very fair white skin made her red freckles show all the more. She was rail thin and was always embarrassed about it. She often wore baggy clothes to try and hide her very slim frame, but she only looked more lost in them than ever.

8

She knew she shouldn't listen to the taunts or take what they said to heart. But, right now, she was having a hard time ignoring it.

She sat down on the stream bank with her chin resting on her knees. The stream widened out and became a green pond with a gigantic willow tree hanging her grass-skirt branches over the edge.

She thought she saw some ducks on the far side and felt in her pocket for a piece of soft pretzel she had not finished at lunch. After being pointed at and laughed at in the cafeteria, she'd lost her appetite. She tore it into pieces and tossed a few into the water, thinking the ducks might see them and check out the water near her for food.

Suddenly, there was the sound of a swish in the water. Something golden leapt out then dived down, snatched a piece of pretzel, and disappeared under the water.

It had all happened so fast! She wasn't exactly sure what she saw. She found she had jumped to her feet as if to run away, but her curiosity got the better of her. She knelt down on the bank to see if she could identify the golden thing that had snatched the snack from the water. A few seconds went by and then, *sploosh!* Up out of the water, the golden fish flew again. It snapped another piece of pretzel and disappeared under the rippling water.

Justine sat back on her heels and smiled in wonder. "What kind of fish was that?"

The golden fish appeared a few more times and finished all the floating pretzel pieces. Justine watched in amazement the whole while with a smile of wonder on her face.

"You don't see *that* every day!" she thought to herself. It was a lucky thing she had a piece of pretzel in her pocket. It was lucky thing she had decided to toss it into the water when she did.

"Must be my lucky day!" she thought to herself with a laugh.

She pulled her drab-brown notebook from her backpack. She was using it as a journal since she moved. She thought it would be neat to write down all the new experiences she would be having and how cool it would be to read later when she was used to the place.

Justine began to read some of the first entries, then a few more, and a few more. Mostly they were all about how she was being tortured by the Cool Girls, being embarrassed by them every day and how that Carl Jones, who followed them around, started his trick of barking at her just to make them laugh.

Justine felt the pain of it all over again and stopped reading. She looked out over the peaceful pond and thought about her "lucky fish."

She decided *not* to write down anything else about the stupid Cool Girls. She was not allowing them into her journal anymore! She would, at least in her journal, not allow them to keep making her feel badly.

This journal was going to be about the *good* things in her life, even if she had to *make* the good things happen to write about! Then she started to write about this pretty pond and the amazing golden fish that came to help her change her life!

CHAPTER TWO

Carp Can Be Beautiful!

hen Justine got home, her dad was cooking dinner on the grill. He wasn't much for "in-house cooking," but he loved to cook on the grill outside.

"Must be the caveman in me, because I do love watching meat sizzle over fire!" he had once proclaimed.

The smell of hot dogs and burgers filled the air with a heavenly scent, and her dad was singing an old song his dad had loved from ancient times. Some of the words went:

> "Hot diggeddy dog diggeddy
> BOOM, what you do to me
> It's so new to me, what you do to me
> Hot diggedy dog diggedy
> BOOM, what you do to me
> When you're holding me tight!"

He really loved the *boom* part and tried to flip the burgers each time he sang it.

"Hey, the most beautiful girl in the world is home!" her father said with a big smile when he saw her coming up the driveway.

She had to smile at that, because it always made her feel good. Even if she didn't always believe it was true, it was nice to know someone did.

She dropped her bag on the picnic table and gave her father a hug, which he gave back along with a kiss on the top of her head.

"Burning burgers?" she asked.

"Not at all," he answered with a miffed air. "I am searing them with expert precision!"

She laughed. "Excuse *me*, Professor! When will they be ready?" Her stomach was grumbling since she ate so little at lunch and the smell of dinner was overpowering.

"Pretty soon," he said turning the hot dogs carefully so they would brown evenly. "How about setting the table for me? Mom should be home any minute now."

"Sure," she said and turned to go into the house.

"How was your day?" he called out as she left.

Before she even thought about it, she called out, "Good." Usually she said it because she did *not* want to talk about the day. Today though, she felt like she meant it. "I found a 'lucky fish,'" she thought, "and I kicked the Cool Girls out of my journal." She was smiling because, somehow, it made her feel powerful.

When they all finally sat down to dinner, Justine asked her dad, "What kind of fish could be in the pond by the park?"

"Hmmmm," he said. He had a mouthful of juicy burger and wanted to enjoy it before swallowing. Justine crunched on some chips while waiting.

Her mom asked, "Were you down there by yourself, honey? I don't think that's such a good idea..."

"I just took a quick walk through on my way home. It was such a nice day..." she answered.

"Bluegills, maybe. Sunnies, little panfish mostly, minnows," her dad answered her after swallowing.

"I just don't like the idea of you in the woods by yourself," her mother continued. "Tell her, Bob."

"Well, it's pretty safe in the park," her father said, "but by the river, I'd like to know you were with someone." He knew the water wasn't really deep, because it was just a stream really, but safety was always important to them.

"Okay," Justine said. "I thought I saw a bigger kind of fish," she continued.

"Really?" her dad said. He thought for a moment. "Carp, maybe? Sometimes they show up in a pond." He wiped his face with a napkin since he loved to overload his burgers with ketchup.

"Justine, I don't want you by the pond alone anymore," her mother continued.

"*Okay!*" Justine said, feeling a little annoyed.

After dinner, Justine finished her homework and was really glad school was almost over because the homework stuff was really a drag.

Then, out of curiosity, she looked up "carp" on the Internet. The description didn't exactly fit what she had seen:

"Two barbels on each side of the mouth. No other species that closely resembles the carp has these barbels. Most carp are bronze-gold to golden yellow on the sides and yellowish white on the belly."

The color sounded about right. And those little whiskers, they must be barbels. Then she followed a link to "ornamental carp," also called koi, and there, she found a picture of her "lucky fish!" She saw beautiful red-and-white ones and black-and-white speckled ones and even calico ones!

She read how they were used in artificial ponds and began to wonder how *this* fish ended up in *her* pond.

She read about how koi fish were considered lucky in China, bringing health, harmony, and happiness.

It struck her funny that when she first saw the koi in the pond, *she* thought that it was lucky too! She looked through the many images of lucky koi in art and found them very beautiful, in a funky sort of way. She chose one and printed it out. She pasted it on the cover of her old, brown journal.

Justine smiled in satisfaction. She was sure that harmony and happiness would be on its way.

CHAPTER THREE

When is a Carp not a Carp?

Pudgy Mason had been watching the new girl, Justine, for weeks. She had seen how Caroline, Samantha, and Roxy, the Cool Girls, had been laying the teasing on her quite heavily. This, sad to say, was a big relief to Pudgy because they were too busy to bully her.

Oh, in the beginning, Pudgy had tried to, let's face it, kiss up to the Cool Girls by running errands, loaning money, handing over homework on occasion. But it never was enough and the taunting would start over again. When they would find her boring after awhile, they would pick on one of the other girls.

While Pudgy did feel sorry for the new girl, she was too happy being left alone to want to help. And even if she *wanted* to help, she had no clue as to *how* to help. Often, at night, she would comfort herself by devising all kinds of plans to humiliate her tormentors by replacing their hairspray with spray paint, or putting spiders in their purses. This only helped for a little while, and really she was too afraid of spiders herself to try.

One day, however, she noticed something different. She was always watching, because you never knew when they would turn on *her* again and she liked to be prepared.

But on this day, something new happened. When the girls began to ask, "Dog Bone, have you visited the pound lately? Oh, I forgot, you might not make it out of there alive!" and finish with taunting laughter, Justine did not turn red or try to yell back or even try to laugh it off the way most of the bullied girls did.

She looked at them, shrugged ever so slightly, and kept walking away as if she hadn't heard anything worth commenting on.

The Cool Girls looked surprised and yelled, "Hey, are you deaf as a dog bone, too?"

But Justine kept on going and walked right up to Mr. Pritchard, the art teacher, who was coming out into the hall, and started talking to him.

The Cool Girls looked a little uneasy at first, thinking Dog Bone was going to snitch on them. But Dog Bone was showing him something, and he smiled as they talked.

The Cool Girls decided to move off just in case. Pudgy watched until Justine finished talking to the art teacher and headed off to class.

She had to admit it was worth seeing the Cool Girls squirm a bit and smiled broadly. She wondered how Justine managed not to fold under the bully tactics and then wondered if the Cool Girls would be worse on her or would they look for a new target. Then her smile faded and she began to prepare for the worst.

Over the next few days, try as they would, the Cool Girls could not get the reaction they wanted from Justine. Samantha, their leader, seemed determined to get the better of her. But Justine always seemed to have something else on her mind and was involved with some sort of project that Mr. Pritchard was advising her about.

Eventually, Samantha gave up, writing Justine off as too dumb to understand, and turned her sights onto Alice, who had recently gotten braces on her teeth. So now it was, "'Metal Mouth,' can you pull in radio stations with those braces?" and, "What would happen if we got a really big magnet?"

Pudgy sighed with relief once again, but she was still curious about Dog Bone and how she had escaped the Cool Girls bullying. One day after school, Pudgy got up the nerve to follow Justine, and maybe even try to strike up a conversation. She was surprised when Justine did not head for home but headed in the direction of the park.

Pudgy followed her, but not too closely. Justine walked on the path around the park for a while, seemingly enjoying the air and the scenery. Then when she reached a huge willow tree, she turned off the path and went toward the stream. Pudgy waited a moment and crept over the bank to find Justine sitting on a ledge overlooking the pond and throwing something into the water.

"Why are you following me?" Justine said to whoever was behind her. She had heard Pudgy's breathing for a while now. Pudgy, true to her nickname, was one who preferred a snack to exercise any day.

Pudgy was shocked but decided to move down to join Justine and explain. "I really wanted to ask you something..." Pudgy began.

"So ask," Justine said simply, not sure whether this was a new ploy of the Cool Girls or what.

"How did you...How did you do it?" she asked lamely, not knowing how to say what she wanted to say.

"How did I do what?" Justine asked in return, baffled by Pudgy's question.

"How did you get the mean girls to leave you alone?" Pudgy asked. Her face was red from strain and embarrassment.

Justine almost wanted to laugh at the question but when she looked at the other girl's chubby, earnest face, she felt sorry for her, knowing she had been a target too.

"What's your name?" Justine asked.

"Mostly ever one calls me Pudgy, even some of the teachers," Pudgy said.

"So I heard, but is that your real name?" Justine asked her, feeling angry with people who stick other people with hurtful names.

"No, it's Elizabeth, but my folks just call me Bess," Pudgy said with a sad smile.

"Well, Bess, I'll tell you. One day I just got tired of letting the bullies get the best of me. I'm not a Dog Bone any more than *you* are a Pudgy."

"Well, I *am* kind of pudgy..." Pudgy said.

"I may be as skinny as a dog bone, but it doesn't mean I *am* one. And those 'Cool Girls' aren't so cool in my book. There is more to us than a name some person slaps on us, and I decided that *they* don't get to say who I am. *I do*," Justine answered with her whole heart and soul.

"So Bess, it's up to you: live by their rules, or live by your own. I don't have to answer to Dog Bone, and you don't have to answer to Pudgy anymore."

"But how do you handle it when they tease you? I watched. You used to shake and blush and stuff..." Pudgy asked sincerely.

"I just pretend they shrink right before my eyes and as they get smaller, their voices get quieter until I just choose not to listen anymore."

"Wow," Pudgy said with wonder. "Do you think it would work for me?"

"I don't know," Justine said truthfully, looking at Bess's hopeful expression. "All I can say for sure is it works for me."

Pudgy was quiet for a moment. She had thought of herself as Pudgy for as long as she had been in school. No one in her family ever called her that though. "Why is it easy to let people call me one thing at home and another in school?" she wondered.

It must have been easy, for she couldn't remember minding it until lately. Pudgy/Bess looked at Justine, who was now gazing at the pond as if she was watching for something.

Suddenly there was a splash and a large, golden fish leapt out of the water, snatched the bread or whatever was floating, and disappeared into the murky pond water.

"What was *that*?" Bess cried out in wonder.

"Well, you might call it a carp because, that's what it basically is, or you might call it an ornamental koi, because that's what it is, too." Justine said with a slight grin.

"Huh?" Bess asked with confusion.

"I choose to call it a koi. The Chinese think they are lucky. I think so too. I think I'd rather call you Bess than Pudgy, if you don't mind, because that's who I think *you* are. And I *really* would *much* rather you call me Justine and not *Dog Bone*," Justine said, smiling at Bess.

"I like Bess better," Bess said. "I don't think I ever have or ever *would* want to call you Dog Bone."

At that very second, they heard another splash. They turned, thinking to see the lucky golden koi again. But this time, it was a *white* koi with red markings leaping high out of the water, snatching a breadcrumb, and disappearing into the pond!

The girls looked at each other with shock and said at the same time, "*There are two!*"

"Well, Bess," Justine said with a smile, "I think we just became the Lucky Koi Club! We may be a couple of carps to the rest of the world, but just between the two of us, I think we are beautiful, ornamental koi!"

CHAPTER FOUR

Carp Have Got To Stick Together

Justine and Bess had managed to withstand the ribbing they got back at school once they decided to hang out together. The Cruel Girls (as they now called them) thought it was hilarious that skinny Dog Bone and chubby Pudgy had decided to team up. "Talk about opposites attracting!" the Cruel Girls laughed in their faces. But they used Justine's technique of shrinking their tormentors down to their proper size and made daily trips to the pond to see their lucky fish. Supporting each other in this way the girls found the taunting a little easier to take.

On eBay, Bess had found lucky koi key chains they could hook on their backpacks to remind them that even if the world thought of them as carp, they were really beautiful koi inside.

At the pond, they talked about what they liked to do and what they wanted to do when they got out of school. They also talked about the others in school who were still at the Cruel Girls' mercy.

"I know that Alice is getting creamed because of her braces," Bess said.

"Jan is getting grief because of the different clothes she wears," Justine added.

"Well, how do we get to them without, you know, embarrassing them or *us*?" Bess asked.

"I guess we could try jumping in when they are being trashed and, you know, rescuing them," Justine said uncomfortably.

"Wow, that could really turn out badly for us if we are caught in the crossfire," Bess said dubiously.

"Or maybe we could catch them right afterward," Justine suggested.

"Well, I guess the only thing we can do is watch for a 'jump-in-able' moment and go from there," Bess said thoughtfully.

Justine saw a chance the next day when Alice was being bombarded with jokes about looking like the grill of a car. She went straight up to a red-faced and tear-stained Alice and said, "The principal wants to see you." The small crowd that had gathered to hear the jokes now all catcalled and "ooo-ed" as if Alice was in big trouble.

Alice turned and followed Justine back into the school and toward the principal's office. Just before they got there, Justine shoved Alice into the girls' bathroom.

"Hey, what's going on?" Alice demanded, rightly confused by the bullying, the summons to the principal's office, and the shove.

"Look, Alice, I don't know how to explain this to you, but Bess and I are tired of watching the others pick on you the way they picked on us," Justine hastily explained.

"Well, at least when they picked on *you*, they left *me* alone!" Alice said miserably as she splashed cold water on her face.

"We don't think they should be picking on any of us," Justine said.

"Yeah, well how are you going to stop that?" Alice asked angrily now.

"We haven't figured it out yet but we're trying too," Justine said lamely.

"Nice…well let me know when you do. I have to see the principal," Alice said sarcastically.

"No, you don't," Justine said, thinking about what Alice said. It was true. They didn't really have a plan.

"What?" Alice now demanded. "I thought you said…" Alice sputtered outraged.

"I only said that to get you out of there," Justine said, her mind trying to grasp an idea.

"Why?" Alice asked in surprise, shoving Justine who was staring straight ahead.

"Why what?" Justine asked sort of stupidly.

Alice rolled her eyes in disbelief. "Why did you pull me away from them?"

"Because you don't deserve to be treated like that, no one does," Justine answered, looking straight at Alice.

Alice took that in, tipping her head to one side, trying to understand what Justine had just said.

"You're right," Alice said finally, looking at Justine with totally agreement.

"If you can, meet Bess and me after school for a while" Justine smiled, sensing success in a bumbling sort of way.

"Bess? Who's Bess?" Alice asked.

"She used to be Pudgy just like *you* used to be Metal Mouth, but now she's Bess," Justine said with a big smile now.

"Like you *used* to be Dog Bone?" Alice asked, smiling now, too.

"That's right, but now I'm Justine."

"Well, Justine, Alice is glad to meet you!"

Bess's rescue of Jan was reversed because Bess was the one under fire at lunchtime when one of the Cruel Girls thought it would be funny to throw food at her in the cafeteria, saying, "Go on, take it, I know you are just dying for more!"

When the girls got up to go, Jan jumped up, picked up the Twinky cupcake Samantha had tossed at Bess, and threw it with all her might at Samantha's head as she left. She missed but she had shocked Bess. Jan went over to her and said, "I'm sorry but I just can't take those people anymore."

Bess smiled and explained to her about how Justine and she felt the same way. She asked Jan to meet them later and she agreed.

When they all met at the pond Justine tossed some bread into the pond and explained how everything got started and how it was time to change the rules a little.

The new girls were surprised when Justine's koi jumped out of the water followed by the red and white one that Bess declared was hers. Then, to everyone's surprise, a new koi, a calico, leaped up next. Colorfully dressed Jan claimed that koi for herself.

A few moments later, a *fourth* koi, gold and blue this time, splashed through the surface of the pond and spun before diving back in.

Alice cheered and clapped her hands. "There's one for *me!*" she hollered happily.

Bess promised to get more key chains when suddenly a fifth koi burst through the surface! This one was white with black spots, like a Dalmatian! Everyone turned and looked at each other.

"How many of these fish are in here?" Alice asked.

"We have no clue," Justine answered honestly.

"Does this mean we'll need to look for another member for the Clan of the Carp?" Bess asked, laughing.

"Perhaps so," Jan said seriously. "Let's keep our eyes peeled."

CHAPTER FIVE

So...Now What?

When the girls met the next day at the pond, they enjoyed seeing their koi leaping as if to welcome them. They magically appeared, almost as though they expected the girls to come.

"So...now what?" asked Jan as she and the others fed their lucky fish.

"What do you mean?" asked Alice, her eyebrows knit together questioningly.

"Well, what are we going to do about the Cruel Girls and the way they treat us?" Jan said, crossing her eyes in frustration because she thought her question was rather obvious.

Bess began to feel a little nervous as she remembered the spider idea...but didn't really want to bring it up.

They all looked at Justine, who was staring out across the water.

"I don't think we should do anything about them..." Justine said, sounding rather distant.

"Well, what's the point of getting together if we're not going to do something?" Alice asked.

"I don't think we should waste any of our time on *them*. The more we think about them, complain about them, hate them, the more they own us. They run our lives."

The rest of the girls were quiet, not knowing what they should say.

"Well, what *should* we do?" Bess asked just to break the silence.

"Follow your bliss!" Jan said all of a sudden.

"Huh?" asked Alice really confused now.

"My sister, she's in college. She says if you want to be happy, you should do the things that make you happy, think about what makes you happy, and—"

"And what?" asked Bess.

"Then you'll be happy! Just follow your bliss!" Jan said triumphantly.

Justine smiled and nodded. "That's it! If we are doing the things that make us happy, the Cruel Girls won't matter!"

"Well, I love making my own clothes. I know they are different and funky-looking, but they're mine! That's bliss for me," Jan said confidently.

"I love to draw," Bess said shyly. She was a little afraid to share something that was important to her. "I don't think I'm really good at it or anything, but I love doing it."

"I can't draw or sew, but I love nature and stuff and I like to take pictures with my camera," Alice said, catching the bravery that was growing around her.

"What about you, Justine? What's your bliss?" Jan wanted to know, a sparkle in her eyes made them shine like the surface of the pond.

Justine had never talked about writing before. She didn't do it very much and didn't know if she was any good at it, but she liked it when she wrote her thoughts down. She had to say something...

"I guess...I guess I like to write..." she said, feeling embarrassed.

"Well, maybe we could share what we do...with each other, you know, when we felt like it?" Bess said hopefully, trying to help this new idea take shape.

"I do it all the time!" Jan exclaimed as she stood up and twirled so that her multicolored skirt flared around her.

The others all laughed, and Jan's calico koi leaped from the water and spun in the air before splashing back into the cool, green water.

CHAPTER SIX

Following Your Bliss

*I*t was the last day of the school year. For the next few months, the girls would be free from the teasing and name-calling. Justine, Jan, and Alice met at the pond. They were in the habit of coming from different directions so as not to tip off anybody that they were meeting.

"Where's Bess?" asked Justine. Bess had always been one of the first to arrive to feed her red-and-white koi. Bess had never had a pet and "Pepper," the red-and-white fish that had reminded Bess of a peppermint candy, was the nearest thing to having one.

"She said something about stopping at the library first," Jan said, slipping off her sandals and letting her toes experience the deliciously cool and tingly water.

"I wouldn't stick my feet in that green water," said Alice, who was a little bit of a germ freak.

Jan looked at the greenish water, and, after a dubious look from Justine, pulled her feet out to air-dry them.

"Is she getting the books for summer reading *already?*" Justine asked, thinking that it was *much* too soon to start prepping for the fall.

"Dunno," answered Alice, who leaned back, breathed in the summer-warmed air, and drank in the peaceful sounds around her.

They heard someone coming, someone in a hurry. It was Bess, puffing and wheezing until she scooted underneath the drooping branches of their weeping willow that hid them from view.

"Hi!" Bess gasped, smiling and her eyes twinkling with excitement. She was clutching a yellow sheet of paper to her chest as if it were a surprise she was waiting to share.

"What's up?" asked Jan, taking in all the signs that there was important news to be heard.

"Well," said Bess glancing around in a way that made all the girls eager to hear, "I stopped at the library because I heard about a way for us to 'follow our bliss' this summer!"

Everybody had quizzical expressions on their faces as Bess just beamed.

"*Okay...*" Justine said. "So tell us, Bess, how can we 'follow our bliss' this summer?"

"Well," she began with a giggle, "I stopped to return a book and saw this!" She held out the yellow flyer for the girls to see.

"Arts Festival!" it proclaimed. Bess was nodding and smiling like crazy.

The rest of the girls looked at each other, not really understanding what Bess was so excited about.

"*This is it!*" she said again waving the paper as if shaking it under their noses would make them understand better.

"It says that," and she turned it around so she could read it to them, "anyone interested in displaying works of art may call Sue at the library and reserve a space."

The girls still stared at Bess as if she had started speaking Swahili.

"All of us like to do something artsy and if we work together, we can make a really nice display!"

"Are you out of your mind?" Alice asked.

Bess's smile evaporated and she looked disappointed.

Jan looked thoughtful and Justine just looked surprised.

"I think you might have a good idea," Jan said, her smile growing bigger by the moment.

Bess's smile began to reappear. "Alice's photography, my drawings, Jan's sewing…." she began a list.

Bess's red-and-white koi leaped from the water, throwing sparkling diamonds of pond water into the warm summer air.

"*Koi!*" called Bess. "We can all work on something that uses *koi* in the design!"

Justine was feeling a little uncomfortable since she didn't have a talent for art you could display, like a picture or a painting.

"So…like…we can each do stuff that has koi and we can display it, together, in a group, right?" Alice said, gesturing with her hands to get a grasp on the idea.

"That's *right!*" cried Bess as the gold-and-blue koi skimmed the surface searching for something to nibble.

Justine was feeling more and more uncomfortable and sat quietly as the others kept chiming in.

Bess noticed Justine and could see something was wrong. She thought for a moment and realized what the problem was.

"Do you think you could write a story about lucky koi? I could draw some illustrations for it. We could even *read* it at the festival, you know, to the kids!" Bess said, hoping to draw Justine back into the group.

Justine was still feeling uncomfortable, but for a very different reason now. While she loved to write down ideas from time to time, she had never written a whole story and didn't even know if she'd be any good at it. "Ummm, maybe…I never did it before…I guess I could try…" she said

"That's the spirit!" cried Jan. Before they left, they made plans to meet at Justine's house the next day to share their work and think about what they might show at the art festival.

Justine walked slowly home, sort of nervously, because she, of all the girls, did not have a clue as to what she might do, and honestly, she was not even sure she really could…

CHAPTER SEVEN

Going With the Flow

The girls arrived the next day armed with examples of their work. Justine welcomed them with pink lemonade and koi-shaped shortbread cookies.

"*Where* did you get these!" cried Jan as she sank her teeth into the soft, sweet-but-salty, buttery, shortbread fish.

"I made them," Justine said proudly. "My mom found the cookie mold online and showed me how to make the shortbread."

Justine's mom, who was working at home for the day, smiled just as proudly at her daughter from the adjoining office room.

After they finished their snack, they spread out Alice's photos from around the pond.

The birds and flowers and the willow tree were quite pretty.

"You certainly have an eye for detail!" said Jan.

"Those birds look like they could fly right off the page," Bess said.

Everyone agreed that each one was a prize. But they asked if she could also capture more koi pictures.

Next came Bess's drawings. Colorful koi seemed to dance across the page. And each drawing was better than the next!

"These are fabulous, Bess!" cried Alice.

"Sheer genious," agreed Jan.

"Stunning!" breathed Justine.

Bess glowed with their praise. "Thank you very much," she said with a big smile and looking away so the girls would not notice her tears of happiness.

"Boy," Jan said, "I wish I could get some of your designs on my clothes."

"Well, you can," said a voice from the next room. Justine's mother came in and said, "You can scan the designs into the computer, print it on transfer paper, then iron the design onto your clothes."

"Really?" all the girls asked together.

"Really," laughed Justine's mom. "I'll pick some up for you tomorrow. And I bet those photos would make great note cards. They have kits to make them at the office supply store, too. Maybe you can make them and sell them at the art festival as a fund raiser."

"Wow, how cool is that!" said Alice with her eyes all round with wonder. "Thanks, Mrs. Richards!"

Justine's mom went into the kitchen and tussled her daughter's hair as she passed by. Justine smiled a crooked smile, half happy about the new ideas and half panicky because she *still* had not come up with an idea she liked for her story.

The girls began to gather their things and promised to meet the next day when Mrs. Richards had picked up the supplies they couldn't wait to try out.

After they left Justine asked her mom how long it would be before dinner.

"Oh, in about an hour and a half or so," her mom answered.

"I'm going for a little walk then," Justine said.

"Okay, just be careful," she said as she stirred the chilli on the stove.

Justine grabbed her koi notebook and pen and headed for the pond. Maybe she could think better outside near her lucky koi because right now, she was feeling like a plain, old carp.

CHAPTER EIGHT

Roxy

Roxy had never felt so bored or so out of sorts in her life. When school let out, her pals flew off for the summer, Caroline to Europe for a tour and Samantha to San Diego visiting her grandparents. Her parents had promised a trip to Banff by train through the Canadian Rockies, but that was not until August, which now seemed a lifetime away.

She was sitting at Chi Chi's Sidewalk Cafe sipping a glass of frozen mint lemonade when she noticed Justine walking by and heading for the park. She and her new friends had been driving Caroline and Samantha crazy because they used to be so easy to tease but lately it wasn't working.

Without an easy target, they seemed to argue with each other a lot more, and that was driving *her* crazy.

"So, where is Dog Bone off to today, I wonder," she thought, smiling slightly. It might be interesting to find out. She waited a bit then got up and followed Justine, keeping her distance so as not to be found out.

Justine did not look around, so Roxy thought she wasn't out for a stroll. In one hand, she carried a brown notebook.

"Could it be a precious journal, writing down all her drab little thoughts?" Roxy chuckled to herself.

As they rounded a large bend in the path, Roxy lost Justine. "Huh?" she thought to herself. "Where did she go?" Roxy peered all around the park that was visible, but no Justine. She began to backtrack and passed a large weeping willow tree. She tried to peek underneath it but was afraid she would be seen.

Then Roxy remembered that there was a bridge further down on the path. "I could cross it and stroll along on the other side. Maybe I'll be able to see her on the bank. With my sunglasses on, she won't be able to tell that I'm looking for her," she thought.

So off she jogged and found the bridge. Her sandals slapped the red wooden floorboards until she reached the opposite side of the stream. Then she started walking along the trail toward where she *thought* she might see Justine.

When she saw the weeping willow, she realized that it was shielding the bank, making it hard to see if Justine was there or not. She felt sort of angry that Dog Bone had made her go through all this trouble and picked up a rock and skipped it across the green pond. A few ducks swimming serenely near the bank quacked loudly in protest and flapped their white wings.

There was no response, so Roxy marched back toward town. What she didn't see in her huffiness was a white koi with black spots following behind her as far as it could go. Then, it jumped out of the water and landed with a huge splash. But Roxy did not look back. She had no interest in slimy, smelly fish.

CHAPTER NINE

Once Upon a Time...

"Once upon a time," Justine had written in her journal. "Well, that's how a story usually starts," she said grumpily to herself. But after that, she was stuck, stuck, stuck.

She fished in her pockets and pulled out a baggie full of fish food she had bought thinking bread was probably not the healthiest thing for her koi to eat. Her shimmering, golden koi was already cruising along the shoreline anticipating his snack.

"There you go, boy," she said, laughing to herself because she hadn't the slightest clue whether it was a boy koi or a girl koi. Then she laughed again at the silly sound of "boy koi."

Some writer I am, she thought suddenly, her smile fading from her lips. "I can't even think of a good name for *you*!" she said to her faithful fish.

She tossed the food in and watched the sparkling water ripple and her koi's mouth gape open and then closed over and over. "Hmmmm...Sparkle...What do you think?" she asked her fish as it munched.

As soon as she said the name, the fish splashed his tail and sent a shower that rained down on Justine. She gasped in shock at first and then she laughed out loud. "That's settled, then, not Sparkle, *Splash!*"

With this, the golden fish baptized Justine again and she laughed a second time.

She moved away from the pond and sat back with the smile still stretched happily across her face. She pulled her journal toward her, picked it up, and began to write:

Once upon a time, near a pretty pond, a weeping girl sat, tears rolling down her face, sobs coming straight from her heart. From beneath the rippling blue water arose a magical golden fish. It watched the sad girl for a while. Then it said, "Girl, sad girl, why do you cry?" The girl did not look up at first. She was shy and did not want to see who it was that had seen her crying so. "I am crying because I am not happy," she said, her voice thick with her feelings.

"Perhaps I can help you," said the magical fish, who was feeling very sorry for her.

The girl looked up to see who the kind person was that cared enough to try to help, but she saw no one!

"Where are you?" she said, feeling very confused. She was sure she had heard someone speaking to her.

"I am here," said the fish.

The girl looked all around, but she saw no one.

"I cannot see you!" she cried. "Please show yourself!"

"But I am here, in the pond," laughed the fish.

"In the pond?" asked the poor girl, now more confused than ever.

"I am a fish," the fish said proudly.

"A fish?" the girl said, not really believing what she was hearing. Then she spotted the shiny, magical, golden fish in the pond. In answer to her question, the fish leaped out of the water and twisted in the air before it landed with a big splash.

Justine read the last sentence out loud then said, "That was for you, Splash!"

Splash just flipped his tail in the air and sent a small fan of droplets flying.

"Why, if you can talk, you must be a magical fish!" the girl cried.

"Indeed I am!" said the bold fish. "But tell me, girl, why do you cry?"

"Oh, I am very sad, dear fish!" said the poor girl.

"What would make you happy?" asked the kindly fish.

Here Justine stopped. She checked her watch and it was almost time for supper! "Uh oh, Mom won't be happy if I'm late!"

She closed her notebook, but now she was smiling. She leaned over the bank to see her lovely, lucky koi still there.

"Thank you, my dear, lucky koi! Thank you for helping me to find my idea!" She blew Splash a kiss and scurried up the bank, skipping almost all the way home.

That night, after supper, Justine worked in her room, thinking and writing, changing her mind, thinking of something better. She wrote down her thoughts that seemed to run fast and far without a stop, as if they had been waiting for her already made.

She could not believe it was eleven o'clock already! The time had flown and she had enjoyed every minute of it. It wasn't easy, but wow, it was sure fun! She gave a mighty yawn and went downstairs to kiss her parents goodnight. As soon as her head hit the pillow, she was fast asleep.

CHAPTER TEN

Finding Happiness

The girls gathered again at Justine's the next day to try out the transfer paper to create T-shirts with Bess's designs. Mrs. Richards helped them get started and once they got the hang of it, they were thrilled with the results.

"I was talking with my Gran, and she said she'd like to teach me to quilt this summer," said Jan. "She's the one who taught me how to sew."

"Hmmmm," said Bess. "Do you think she could make a koi quilt?"

For a moment the question kind of hung in the air while each girl's brain began to spin.

Jan's mouth hung open in surprise then her eyes grew wide. She smacked her forehead with her hand and said, "Bess, you are a genuis!"

"My math teacher doesn't think so," Bess said a little glumly as she gingerly pulled the paper off and looked at her lovely red-and-white carp on her blue T-shirt.

"I can help you with that," said Alice. "I love math."

"Bess!" said Jan. "Your idea about a koi quilt! We could all work on it together—"

"And we can make patches with our picture transfers of our koi!" chimed in Justine.

"Wow, that would really be unique!" said Mrs. Richards.

"One of a kind!" Alice joined in.

"Hey, I *am* a genuis!" laughed Bess.

"I'll talk to my Gran and find out what we need to start," said Jan.

"Since I'm being such a genius, I have something else to ask you," said Bess, smiling.

Everyone one looked at her expectantly. Suddenly, she felt amazed. For most of her life she had felt, well, dumb. Most people either teased her about her weight or about not being so smart in math and *nobody*, aside from her family, had ever really listened to her ideas before, let alone think they were any good. She felt her heart squeeze with happiness, then sighed.

"Well?" said Jan, who liked snappy answers.

"Sue, at the library, is looking for volunteers to read stories to the little kids during the week. I thought if each of us took a day, well, it would be a good thing," Bess said hopefully and with her fingers crossed behind her back.

"What a nice idea, Bess!" Mrs. Richards said.

"I wouldn't mind," said Justine.

"You can count me in," said Jan heartily.

"Do…do you think it will be okay, with my braces and all?" Alice asked doubtfully.

"You speak quite clearly, Alice," said Mrs. Richards with a smile.

"Mmm, okay, I'll give it a try," said Alice, still a little unsure about how it would work out. Being teased by kids your own age is one thing, being teased by little kids, that would be devastating.

"We could all go and, you know, give each other moral support," Bess suggested.

"That would help," Alice smiled gratefully.

One afternoon as they were sitting near the pond lazily enjoying a perfect summer day, Bess asked, "So, Jus, how's that story coming?"

Justine jumped a little. She was so intent on her story that she forgot where she was and that she was not alone.

"Oh, well, mmm, fine, almost finished, I think..." Justine said in a stumbling way.

"So when are you going to share it with us?" Jan asked, sitting up straight from her reclining position and looking Justine right in the eye.

"Well, it has a few kinks in it yet and...a couple more days and I should be done, I think," Justine said, trying to sound confident.

"Yeah, I'm dying to hear it," Alice said, wiping her lips delicately, for the braces made her mouth drool a little from time to time.

"I'll work on it hard tonight and see how far I can get," promised Justine, who was also making the promise to herself as well as to her friends.

After the "Koi Girls," as her father called them, left, Justine ran up to her room and pulled out her journal. She reviewed what she had written so far and smiled slightly as she read:

"What would make you happy?" asked the kindly fish. "Oh, if only I could be beautiful, then I would be happy!" cried the girl. Beautiful people always seemed so happy to her.
"Ah," said the fish. "Easy enough! Come close to my pond, dear girl, and wash your face and you will be beautiful!"
"Truly?" cried the girl.
"Truly, dear one, just wash!" answered the magical fish, and he flipped his tail and splashed her.
The girl washed quickly and her face became very fair to behold. She peered at herself in the pond and gasped with joy.
"Oh, dear fish! How can I thank you?" cried the girl.
"Go and be happy, if you can," said the kindly fish.
A few weeks later, the girl returned to the pond. Her beautiful face was as sad as ever. She sat at the edge of the pond. Her tears caused ripples on the peaceful pond's surface.

As if in answer to a call, the golden, magical fish suddenly appeared and looked with sorrow at the beautiful girl.

"What? Tears again? Dear girl, didn't being beautiful make you happy?" asked the magic fish.

"Oh, magic fish! Being beautiful was wonderful for a while. Everyone complimented me and wanted to be my friend, but then my old friends did not feel comfortable with me. They said I thought I was too good for them.

"Others said I was a show-off and would never really be as good as they were. And so now, dear fish, I have no friends and am sadder than I was before!"

The fish looked at the very sad girl and said kindly, "Do not cry, dear one, for you have learned something very important. Looking beautiful will not make you happy."

"Well, then," said the girl, "perhaps if I were rich. Then I would get all the things my heart desires and then I would be happy!"

"Ah, rich is what you want! Easily done!" cried the magical fish. It disappeared under the shimmering surface of the pond for a few moments as the girl waited, full of excitement.

When it reappeared, it held an ancient coin in its mouth and swam near the girl. She reached out and took the coin.

"This coin will bring you a fortune," said the fish with a wink. "Go, become rich and be happy, if you can."

So the girl thanked the fish and ran off sure that she would be happy forever!

A month later, the girl was once again crying at the shore of the lovely blue pond.

The magical fish appeared again and sighed. "Ah, my dear one, being rich did not make you happy?"

"Oh, kind fish, at first it was glorious, buying everything I wanted. But soon I grew weary of shopping and had so many things that I didn't want anything else, and I became sad once more."

"I understand," said the fish. "But don't cry! You have learned something very important! Being rich and having many things does not make you happy."

"Perhaps if I had a great talent and became famous!" said the girl excitedly. "Yes, I'm sure that would make me happy!"

"Ah, I see! What would you like to do?" asked the golden fish.

"I know how to play the lute a little and I sing a bit, too," she said.

"Easily done," said the fish. "Come close and rub your fingers over my scales then rub them over your lips," said the fish.

And so she did.

"Now go and see if being famous can make you happy!" cried the fish.

"Oh, thank you, thank you, dear and kind fish!" said the girl, her heart almost bursting with gratitude.

The magical fish watched as its young friend ran from the pond and began to wait for her return.

It was two months later when she finally returned, but she was not crying now. She sat quietly on the shore of the pond. The magical fish had just leaped from the water to catch a bug when it saw her.

"Dear friend, you have returned!" the fish exclaimed. "Tell me, have you become happy?"

"Well," said the girl with a deep, heartfelt sigh. "For a while I was deliriously happy," she began. "Everyone one said I had the most perfect talent in the world. People would come from everywhere to hear me play and sing. They would clap and cheer. It was all very thrilling. But one day I made a mistake. People began to grumble and said, 'She's not so perfect after all. They stopped coming and soon I was forgotten."

"Ah, said the fish, "I understand, but you are not crying."

"No," said the girl, "I am not crying. Now I am wondering."

"What are you wondering, dear one?" said the glittering fish.

"If being beautiful or rich or famous cannot make me happy, what will?" she asked with an open heart and ready to listen.

"I cannot tell you what will make you happy," said the fish wisely.

"Oh…" said the girl, feeling tears beginning to rise.

"But, can you tell me, have you ever been happy?" asked the fish.

"Umm, let me think," said the girl, brushing away her tears quickly and trying hard to think. "Well, I used to like to play my lute and sing to my family, before I was famous. I suppose I was happy then," she said.

"Go, dear one, and do that for a week and come see me again," said the fish.

A week later she came, not crying and not wildly excited but smiling calmly.

She tossed some breadcrumbs on the water and when the magical fish rushed up to snap at them, it was glad to see her.

"You have come! How are you feeling today?" asked the fish.

"I don't feel like crying anymore and I did enjoy playing and singing for my family. They liked it too," she said.

"How nice," said the fish.

"What should I do now?" asked the girl.

"What else do you like to do?" asked the fish in return.

"I liked to dance with my friends," said the girl quickly.

"Go then and dance with your friends for a week and then come and see me," said the fish.

The girl looked a little troubled, since she had not been with them for a while, but she did as the fish said.

A week later she returned, looking calm and satisfied. This time the fish was looking for her and when it saw her coming, he flipped out of the water and splashed a great splash.

"So, dear one," said the fish, "how did it go?"

The girl sat on the bank and looked seriously at the fish. "At first, my friends did not want to dance with me. They said, 'Aren't you too beautiful and too rich and too famous to dance with the likes of us?' But I made them see that I did not care about all of that anymore. I told them I just wanted to be me and wanted to be their friend and wanted to dance with them as we used to."

"After a while, they saw that I had changed and they let me dance with them again," said the girl, ending with a smile.

"Ah, dear one, I am glad," said the magical fish. "You have learned an important lesson. Can you tell me what it is?" asked the fish with a wise wink.

The girl sat and thought for a long moment. Then she said, "There is nothing that can make you happy, because happy does not come from the outside. But you can be happy when you are just yourself doing the things you like. Is that it?" she said shyly and looking at the fish, hoping it would say she was right.

"And are you happy now, dear one?" asked the fish.

"I think I am," said the girl with a sigh of contentment.

"Then I think you have found your answer at last!" said the wise, golden, shimmering, magical fish.

Justine sat back, feeling quite happy herself, now that her story was finished. She had enjoyed every minute that she spent writing it. She was very satisfied with how it had come out in the end and she felt that *she* had learned the lesson the girl in the story had learned. What could be better than that! She could not wait until tomorrow when she would share her story with her friends!

CHAPTER ELEVEN

Lessons Learned

*I*t was around ten in the morning when Justine and her friends headed to the pond. They were all excited about hearing Justine's story. Bess knew that Justine was feeling very nervous about sharing what she wrote, but she also knew that Justine had been working very hard on it and had poured her whole heart and soul into it.

"Oh, I hope it is good," Bess thought. "But even if it is not the greatest story in the world, we have to show her how proud we are that she tried."

When they arrived they ducked under the long, draping willow branches and as if they had heard them coming, their lucky koi began to appear at the water's edge, some jumping and splashing, some waiting patiently for the snacks the girls would bring.

"So, how's the writing going?" asked Jan, who was always pretty straightforward. No beating around the bush for Jan.

Justine's great blue eyes sparkled with excitement and she giggled a little nervously. "I think it's done and," she paused, taking in a little breath and holding it for a second, "and I think…it's good." She hoped she didn't sound too boastful.

They settled into comfortable spots and Justine opened up her journal with the koi on the front. "*The Girl and the Magical Fish*," she began, her heart beating faster.

Her friends sat around her, listening carefully, while the lucky koi swam in the pond near them. They all liked the idea of the story since the koi pond and their individual fish meant a lot to each of them.

They didn't notice that there were other ears listening to the fish tale. Nearby, crouched Roxy, who thought this would be the perfect time to find out what was in that stupid notebook Justine was always carrying around. Since she had found the spot where the girls met, she had been hiding out; trying to figure out what was so special about it.

This was the first time she was able to get close enough to hear them, and it was the first time she saw the koi close up. She was amazed by how beautiful they were. She was amazed that such pretty fish were in this gross, green pond. She was amazed at how tame the fish were. And she was slightly jealous that they didn't seem interested in her at all. "It's probably because they feed them all the time," she thought logically.

Before long, she was just as immersed in the fairy tale as the others were and some of the things made her almost laugh.

"Of course being beautiful, rich, and famous *made* you happy," she thought. As a member of the Cool Girls, she was all of those things. Well, maybe she wasn't famous…but at least popular, which was almost the same thing.

"It's because Justine is *none* of those things that she wrote that story," Roxy thought with a smirk.

When Justine was finished, she looked at her friends, afraid to see fake approval on their faces.

"Oh, Jussy," cried Bess, "that was great!" She had been practicing saying it in her head, but now she said it from her heart.

"Perfect, just perfect! You hit it right on the head!" Alice said, smiling and nodding with agreement.

"It sounds just like one of the stories we read to the kids at the library!" said honest Jan. "Plus, they might learn something too!"

"You really liked it?" asked Justine. Tears of happiness made her eyes glisten.

All the girls said they did and hugged her to prove it.

Something about their actions tugged at Roxy's heart for a moment. The Cool Girls never seemed that...close. They were never really interested in what *you* liked to do. They were only interested in what they thought made them look cool.

Roxy listened to the girls as they excitedly made plans for all their projects. Geeks though they were, they still seemed... shoot...They actually seemed happy!

"How is it possible that geeks could be happy?" Roxy thought sourly.

When the girls left, Roxy sneaked into the Koi Girls' meeting place and sat next to the pond. She found some crumbs of bread and threw them into the water, expecting the fish to rise to get them.

Not one came. Now Roxy felt disappointed and unsettled. She missed being a member of a group with her friends away and now she was looking at her friends in a new way which made her feel uncomfortable too.

"Darn that Justine and her quirky ideas anyway!" she thought and threw a rock into the water very hard.

Then, a strange thing happened. From under the green water came a black-and-white koi. It did not jump or splash. It did not swim around. It stayed in one place as if it were looking right *at her*!

She suddenly felt guilty for throwing the rock. "I…I… I'm sorry," she stuttered to the fish. She felt ridiculous talking to a fish, but after the story and everything, it seemed like the thing to do.

For a few eerie moments, the fish just hung there in the water, giving her the willies in the worst way. Then she snatched up some bread from the ground and tossed it into the water, thinking that is what it wanted. Still it hung there in the water, its fins moving but keeping it in one place. Then its mouth began to open and close.

Roxy began to feel afraid and thought it was going to talk to her like the fish in the story. Perhaps it would be mad at her and tell her off for being such a jerk: throwing in the rock when she knew fish were swimming there!

Suddenly, it disappeared under the water and a moment later it sailed out, water sparkling in the midday sun. Then it made a huge splash as it hit the pond throwing water all over Roxy!

"Hey!" she cried out, shielding her face from the spray. The Dalmatian koi repeated his act several times, until Roxy started to laugh at its antics. "All right already!" she said laughing. "I said I was sorry!"

Then the fish gulped down the bread, and flipped its tail at her as if to say, "Thanks!"

All the other koi appeared and joined the black-and-white one as if welcoming her to their crew. She stayed under the willow for a while, watching the koi and thinking about the story and a lot of other things. She felt like she had to discover what she liked to do so she could *be* happy, too.

Before she left, she found a bookmark on the ground with a 3D picture of a golden koi. She figured it must be Justine's, probably from her journal. She looked at it for a while not really thinking about anything, then she slipped it in her pocket and began to leave the willow. She cast one more glance at the pond. Only her black-and-white koi was left.

"See ya, Spot," she called gently. Spot flipped his tail and disappeared from view under the water.

CHAPTER TWELVE

Cruel Girl to Carp

Justine walked back toward the library shaking her head in total disbelief. It could not be true! She had gone off with her friends. But when she realized that her bookmark was missing, she came back to the protective willow tree only to find one of the Cruel Girls sitting there!

Then, adding insult to injury, she saw the black-and-white koi making *contact* with *her* and even more confusing, she saw the rest of the koi...welcoming her!

Justine felt as if the earth had just turned upside down and spun sideways! She watched as the Cruel Girl picked up her bookmark and wandered away.

"It can't be...it just can't be," Justine kept repeating to herself. "Could *she* be the *fifth* Koi Girl?" she wondered. Then she thought of what she had seen and realized it must be true but... how was this going to work?

Justine's brain pondered this all the way to the library but no answers came to her. Story time had begun. There was a group of about fifteen young kids all gathered around the Story Time Corner, featuring Alice.

In the beginning, Alice was very concerned about her braces being a problem, but as time went on, she discovered that she had a gift for inventing voices for the characters that the kids just loved! Today she was wearing a pointy hat with a long, gauzy veil dangling from the top, like a damsel in the story. The kids were glued to Alice's every word as visions of castles and knights and dragons filled their imaginations.

Justine sat down near Bess, who was grinning from ear to ear enjoying watching and listening to Alice as much as the kids. "She's *good!*" Bess whispered to Justine.

"Yes, yes she is," mumbled Justine, still reeling from what she had seen at the pond.

Bess noticed Justine's less-than-enthusiastic answer. "Hey, what's with you?" she asked.

Justine looked over at Bess, not knowing what to say, where to start, so she just said, "I'll tell you later."

Bess looked at Justine and got a queasy feeling deep in her stomach and was sure that *something* was wrong. This made her feel quite sad. These last few weeks, sharing with the other girls had been *so* great. In the back of her mind, in a small corner, was a quiet dread that one day it would all be over. Justine's upset look made that quiet dread a little louder.

It was then that Justine noticed that Cruel Girl, Roxy, had come in and was listening to Alice, too. Justine's stomach twisted into a knot. She hoped Roxy wasn't here just to gather ammunition to fire at Alice someday, something to make fun of her.

After Alice finished her story to great applause, they headed toward Jan's grandmother's house where they had been working on the koi quilt.

Then, something totally unexpected happened. Roxy was following them, gathering the nerve to speak.

"Justine?" she called.

All the girls froze in their tracks then slowly turned. Justine took a deep breath and walked warily toward her, tossing her red hair out of her eyes, trying to look confident and fearless.

"You called me?" Justine said, waiting to hear some unkind remark or verbal punch.

"I...I found this and I think it belongs to you," Roxy said uncertainly. She held out the bookmark so Justine could take it.

"Uh, thanks," Justine said.

"No problem...it's nice, the bookmark," Roxy said, trying hard to seem friendly.

"Well, thanks," Justine said, eying Roxy suspiciously.

"The fish are pretty neat, too," Roxy ventured, speaking more quietly.

At this, Justine's head snapped up and looked Roxy full in the face. For a moment she thought maybe Roxy would try to hurt them. But Roxy's face was still open and friendly and this confused her even more.

"They really are," Justine said in the same quiet voice, trying to send all her love and concern for the koi in one searching look.

"Maybe…maybe…" Roxy said, afraid to continue even though she wanted to in the worst way.

Justine saw Roxy struggling and wondered if this was the same proud, harsh girl that had laughed at her, behind her back or even in her face.

"Maybe what?" Justine asked.

Roxy took a deep breath and finished, "Maybe, you'd let me join you when you see the fish…sometime."

For the second time that day, Justine was so shocked at the turn of events she hardly could speak.

Roxy took the silence as a good thing and tried one thing more. "I really liked your story, too." Roxy smiled and nodded, trying to show Justine she meant it.

Justine was flabbergasted, kind of embarrassed, and a little angry. She didn't mind sharing with her friends, but with an enemy? But Roxy looked like she meant what she said.

"You did?" was about all Justine could get her mouth to say.

"Yes, I did. It sounded like a real fairy tale, with a good message and all," Roxy said, now with a smile.

"Well, thanks," Justine said with a little smile of pride lighting her face. Then she looked over her shoulder. "I gotta go now."

"See ya?" Roxy said like a question.

"Um, yeah, see ya," Justine answered.

She rejoined her friends who were dying to know what *that* was all about.

Justine was quiet as they walked toward Jan's grandmother's house. "I'll tell you when we get inside," she said, stalling for time.

Once there and sipping the lemonade Jan's grandmother served them, Bess could no longer contain herself.

"*Jus...tell us!*" she cried.

Alice and Jan sat on the edge of their seats eager to hear as well.

"I know..." Justine began, looking around at her friends, "I know who the fifth Koi Girl is."

CHAPTER THIRTEEN

Sharing Your Bliss

Justine shared the whole story with her friends, who sat around her with faces filled with surprise and confusion and suspicion.

"Don't you think this whole thing is just a little bit *weird?*" asked Jan with one eyebrow arched and a sharp edge to her words.

"Not so *weird* when you figure in the fact that all the other Cruel Girls are out of town and *she's* all by herself and probably looking for someone to hang with," said Alice, smiling and nodding in a sly way.

"Maybe she's just looking for things to…to tell the others when they get back so they can embarrass us later," said Bess with the specter of the bullying rising up before her mind's eye.

Justine looked at all her friends and had to admit that everything they said might be true. But something was nagging at her, a feeling that maybe they should let Roxy have a chance. She wasn't sure why. Maybe it was because of the koi and how *they* seemed to accept her. But was it a good idea to base an important choice like this on something as silly as believing in lucky fish?

She could see they were all waiting for her opinion and she felt uncomfortable being on the spot before it was even clear in her own mind, but she decided to try. Maybe by explaining it to somebody else she'd understand it herself.

She took a deep breath and said. "I think we should give her a chance."

"Why? Whatever chance did she ever give to us!" shot back Alice, whose memories of the teasing were still very fresh and painful.

"Let Jus say what she's thinking," said Bess. "Go ahead, Jus," she encouraged.

"I know how mean they've been to us. I know there's a good chance that they will be mean again. But things can't ever change if we don't let them. We still have each other. We know how to deal with them now. If Roxy has come over to our side, that's one less Cruel Girl to deal with. If not, well, then nothing is really lost. We're still us, right?" Justine looked around hoping to see some understanding, only barely understanding it herself.

Bess looked as though she was trying hard to figure out what Justine meant. Alice's face was still pink from remembering those dark days of dealing with the mean things that were said and done to her.

Jan was looking at the quilt they were working on, running her hand over the patch with her calico koi as if she expected *it* to answer the question in her mind. She also looked at the corner where the last fish, Roxy's fish, would go. Then, suddenly, she said, "Okay, I'll give her a chance."

Alice's eyes grew very wide. "Why should we?" she said harshly.

Jan pointed to the Dalmatian koi patch. "If this is *her* fish, then she should have a chance to belong."

They all looked at the quilt, which meant the world to them. Justine's golden koi was in the center because it had been the first. Each of the other girl's koi had a corner.

"I agree," said Bess softly and with a shiver, as if she had just had a revelation and understood something bigger than the regular, ordinary, everyday stuff.

Alice stared at the quilt. Feelings were swirling around inside of her and she wasn't sure which was right or which would win in the end. She ran her hand over her koi, her beautiful blue-and-gold koi, the most exotic of them all, she had thought, as if it would help her see what everybody else saw.

"All right," Alice said solemnly. "I'll give her a chance, but I don't trust her and I don't know if I ever will," she said plainly.

Justine smiled gently. "That's a start."

Alice didn't smile but began working on her patch of the quilt as Granny brought in some blueberry muffins for the girls to share and praised them on their handiwork, which made all of them, even Alice, feel better.

CHAPTER FOURTEEN

Koi is a Way of Life

The next day, when the girls went to the park and arrived at the pond, they found Roxy already there. She was sitting under the protective branches of the willow tree, tossing bits of something into the pond.

The girls stopped short when they saw her and watched the black-and-white koi leaping up occasionally to nab the bits as they floated in the water. It was very plain to all that this carp had chosen Roxy, just as the others had chosen each one of them.

Bess smiled slightly, amazed as always that this wonderful thing had happened to *her* when she never thought something this special ever would.

Jan nodded her head as if to say, "Yep, it's true! *Roxy is* a Koi Girl after all!"

Alice stood very still, fists clenched at her side, not willing to give in just yet. "People can't change that fast, that easy!" she said staunchly to herself.

It was Bess that broke the standoff by saying, "Hi, Roxy!" in the most pleasant voice she could bravely muster.

"Oh, hi Pu…uh…Bess, right?" she stumbled, almost saying the name she had been calling Bess for years. She was blushing, realizing how her words had so often hurt the girl now standing before her.

"That's right," said Alice icily.

"Look, I don't know *how* to apologize for everything I said and did, except to say I was stupid and mean and I'm sorry…" Roxy blurted out, meaning every word she said and yet feeling her pride, of all things, flare up.

"You think it's that easy? I'm sorry? That's it?" Alice demanded, her voice growing louder.

Justine did not want this to blow up into a fight but had no clue as to how to stop the train wreck that seemed about to happen.

"I know it's not enough…" Roxy said, her arms held out with palms up in a "what do you want from me" gesture.

"I really want you to know how I felt, how we *all* felt, while you guys got off on humiliating us for laughs. I guess I want *you* to feel as bad as *that*," Alice said loudly, her breath quickening.

Roxy's hands were down at her sides now and she was blushing furiously. Looking at Alice's pained and tear-stained face made her realize just how wrong she had been.

"If I could, I would," Roxy said quietly, "but, Alice … I *swear* it won't happen again."

Alice was breathing hard, and she swiped away the tears with the back of her hand.

Roxy moved toward Alice (which was a brave thing to do right then) and reached out and hugged her. "I'm so sorry, Alice. I really am," Roxy said.

Everybody else just froze, not sure what would happen next.

After a moment or two, Alice pulled away and said, "Okay, then," as she sniffed and searched for a tissue in her pocket.

"Okay!" Roxy said with a smile. Alice tried to smile, too, after blowing her nose.

"Okay!" said Justine, letting out the big breath she hadn't realized she was holding.

"Okay!" chimed in Jan and Bess, who took turns hugging Roxy.

From behind them they heard splashing sounds and when they turned, they were greeted by their koi in all their individual glory.

Over the next few days, the girls brought Roxy up to speed on everything they were doing. Roxy joined in when she could and seemed to enjoy it all.

"So," Bess asked one day, not long after they had been together, "what is it that *you* like to do, Roxy?"

"I was afraid you'd ask me that," said Roxy with a shy smile.

"Why afraid?" asked Jan as she crunched on an apple.

"Because, I don't really know," she said with a sigh. "I've been doing the things that the other girls told me I should do and never really thought about what I wanted. I guess I was just too...too...lazy to think about what I wanted. And maybe too afraid that, you know...they would..." she paused, blushing again.

"Laugh at you or call you stupid..." said Justine quietly, finally realizing that bullies even bullied each other.

"Well, think about when you were a kid. Was there anything fun that you liked to do?" Alice asked, trying to be helpful.

Roxy was quiet for a while. She did like to shop, but even that got boring after a while. She did like trying on makeup, but you could only put so much on your face. "Hmmm, when I was a kid...Well, I used to have a lot of fun baking cookies with my grandpa until he moved to California," Roxy said. "But no one cooks in my house now except our chef, and he does not like a helper..."

"My mom loves to cook," cried Bess, "and she loves helpers! Maybe she can help you can bake up some of those koi shortbread cookies Jus made for our exhibit!"

"You really think she would?" Roxy asked with surprise and excitement.

"You bet!" Bess said with a wide grin. "I'll ask her when it would be okay and then you'll have the best time!"

"As long as we get samples!" Jan declared.

"When are you going away on your trip?" asked Alice.

Roxy felt a little hurt, like Alice was still mad at her and wanted her out of the close group of friends.

"Right after the art festival," Roxy said with a sad look on her face. "Why?"

"Because I think we're going to miss you, especially if you can bake cookies!" she said with a laugh.

CHAPTER FIFTEEN

Full Bloom

The day of the festival brought with it the most spectacular weather for July. The temperature was warm but not too hot. The sky was bright blue with hardly a cloud. A light breeze was tickling the fully green trees occasionally, and they swayed slightly as if in delight. The town looked cheerful with banners proclaiming that the great day had come.

The girls met at the pond beneath the sheltering willow, which rustled gently as though it were filled with excitement, too.

"We have to have everything set up by one," Jan said, looking down at a list she had put together the night before.

"Right, if we meet at our site by noon, we should be ready," said Alice.

"Oh, I can't wait to see everything all set up, can you?" Bess fairly squealed with excitement.

"Easy there, Bess! You'll burn out before we even get started," Roxy chuckled.

Justine was flipping through one of the copies of her koi fairy tale her mom had made for her. Alice had gotten a gorgeous photo of her golden koi and Bess had hand-lettered the title for her book cover. Justine was nervous about reading it to others, but last night when she read it to her parents, they seemed to like it a lot and said they were very proud. Her dad said he'd hang it on the fridge, but it was too big. They all laughed at that.

By one o'clock, everything was set and when people came by, they gave many compliments and often told others, "Go and see that Koi Girls exhibit!" Alice and Bess sold all their note cards and even took an order for several sets when all the ones on hand ran out.

The cookies were snatched up by the children, many of whom knew the girls from the library. When the judging time came, the Koi Girls' quilt won a prize for best new entry. They looked proudly at their yellow ribbon. They had decided to donate their quilt to the library for display, along with the money they collected from the note cards and cookies.

Justine watched the glow on her friends' faces as they laughed and giggled and thought how much better this summer turned out because of a lucky fish. It was her turn to read her story as the children gathered on the grass outside the library.

Justine began her story with a nervous quiver in her voice. But when she saw their young faces soaking up the story as she read, she felt the awesome power and responsibility that is part of telling a tale to children.

Bess and Jan smiled at each other knowingly as Justine grew more confident and told the story with love.

Alice suddenly looked at Roxy when Justine came to the part where the girl had to go back to her old friends and at first, they did not accept her. She realized how happy she was that she gave Roxy a chance. It would have been a great loss not to have her as a friend. Somehow Roxy knew what Alice was thinking and gave her a wink. Friends can do that from time to time...

When it was all over, they took down their items with bittersweet care, because that which they most desired was now gone. But the friendship they now shared... that could last for a long, long time—maybe always.

CHAPTER SIXTEEN

Forever Koi

Roxy was finishing her cereal one morning after returning from her train trip. It had been exciting, and she had brought back lots of photos to share with the girls. Alice pored over them and proclaimed that they were quite good and that she couldn't wait to travel the world taking pictures of everything!

Her father was reading the paper across from her. He would be leaving soon to start his busy day. He refolded his paper and when Roxy glanced up, she saw something that almost made her choke!

There was a picture of guys around a digging machine posed for a picture. The title of the story said, "Revitalization of the Park Stream and Pond Set to Begin." She strained to read the article that told about how the stream needed to be dredged and the pond cleared of carp, which were stirring up the muddy bottom and killing the plant life.

Suddenly Roxy felt shaky with a kind of fear she never felt before.

"Daddy," she said.

"Hmmmmm?" her father answered absently, his mind on what he was reading.

"*Daddy,*" she said a little louder and with a sharper edge to her voice.

Her father lowered the paper slightly to look at his daughter, alerted by the change in her voice.

"What is it, Roxy?" he asked.

"Daddy," she said again, this time her voice sounded a little quivery with emotion, "I need you to help me with something."

Now, in the past, Roxy had asked for *many things,* usually in a whinny voice, like a child, wheedling for something like a toy, game, or treat. But the sound of her voice, the serious look on her face, and her request for "help" made him put the paper down and look right at her with full attention.

"Is there something wrong, honey?" he asked, now fully curious.

"Yes," she said, "and I think *you* are the only one who can help."

Later that morning, Justine, Bess, and Alice had walked to the park to enjoy one of their last days of freedom before school started. When they got there, they were shocked to find machines and people and TV cameras filming the work that was going on. The area where they had sat beneath the huge willow tree was blocked off and they were not permitting people into the work area.

The girls were frantic to find out what was going on and what had happened to their fish! Jan was brave enough to stop one of the workers who told her the river had too much silt on the bottom and had to be cleaned out so that it would not flood. When she asked about the fish, he said he didn't know about fish, but that they would be finished in a few days and it would be better than before.

Bess was crying, wondering how something so awful could have happened! "You don't think they killed them, do you?" she half-sobbed, tears coursing down her face.

Jan looked very pale and said very coldly and flatly, "It's possible."

Justine felt sick to her stomach and had no words to say.

Alice dabbed her eyes and trembled a little. "Is there anything we can do?" she whispered a few times, but no one answered.

"I wonder what happened to Roxy," Justine said aloud, knowing how awful she was going to feel too.

"She said she was going to meet us here. I guess something must have come up," Alice answered, still talking in a hushed voice.

"You girls better move on out of there, before you get hurt," one of the working guys called out to them.

"Come on, we'll go to my house," Justine said.

The girls turned slowly and sadly and walked to Justine's house, saying over and over things like, "I just can't believe this!"

"Do you think the koi will be all right?" "What's going to happen to them now?"

Justine's dad was off that day and was washing his car in the driveway, singing an ancient Bobby Darin song as he rubbed and scrubbed:

"They was a-splishin' and a-splashin',
Reelin' with the feelin',
Moving and a-groovin,
Rockin' and a-rollin', yeah!"

As he sang, he danced around with a big foamy sponge, soaping up the car until it was all bubbly before he hosed it down. The sight of this grown man singing and dancing and covered with soapsuds made the girls giggle for a moment in spite of the tragedy they had discovered.

He looked up suddenly, saw the girls, and looked very embarrassed. "Uh…hi girls, just thought I'd wash the car…it's such a nice day and all."

Then he noticed Bess's red eyes and their generally depressed faces and asked, "What's up?"

"Oh, Daddy…" Justine started feeling like she was six and wanting him to make everything better.

"It's a long story, Mr. Richardson," Jan butted in, knowing how *her* father hated to be interrupted when washing the car. "It gets all streaky!" he would say.

Mr. Richardson said, "Go into the house and get something to drink and I'll be right in."

Justine smiled gratefully, and the girls went in and poured some lemonade. When Mr. Richardson came in, they explained the whole story and he nodded as they spoke, his face grimacing with understanding.

"I'll make a few phone calls and see if I can find out something, okay?" he said.

"Thanks, Daddy," Justine said, a little spark of hope burning dimly in her heart.

After a while he came into the living room where they were sitting. He sat down near them and sighed. When Justine saw his face and heard his sigh, the little flame of hope just about went out.

"Well, girls, I called around and found out that the city needed to dredge the silt out of the bottom of the stream and pond because if they didn't, the stream might flood if bad rains came. Once they take some of the sludge out of the bottom, the stream would be able to hold more water because it would be deeper."

"But what about our fish?" Bess asked with tears welling up in her eyes again.

Mr. Richardson looked at them sadly and said, "From what I understand, they were removed because they were disrupting the balance of life in the pond..." He explained how carp are usually bottom feeders and how they can cloud up the water when they are searching for food and it makes it hard for the plants to grow. They die and then the fish that use them for food die.

"It's the whole food-chain thing..." Justine said flatly, never realizing until just now how important all that stuff they learned in science could really be.

"But what happened to them?" Bess sobbed.

Mr. Richardson patted Bess on the back and said the person he talked to didn't know. He told the girls how sorry he was and that if he found out more, he'd let them know.

Each girl sat quietly thinking about their own special koi.

"I wonder where Roxy is," Justine asked again.

"Oh, maybe she went back to her rich, 'cool' girlfriends!" Bess said miserably.

"Well, that's a nasty thing to say!" Alice said, feeling shocked and a little angry.

"Why would you say such a thing?" Jan asked.

"Because the koi are gone, maybe she's gone; maybe you'll all go now!" Bess cried.

"Bess, you're hysterical! Just calm down and don't talk when you're so upset! People can be hurt when you talk like that!" Justine told her.

"Or mad!" said Alice.

"Now *you* hate me!" moaned Bess.

"Bess," Justine said as she knelt down beside her sobbing friend. "Look, you're just upset about the koi and its making everything you are afraid of come out."

"I thought the fish were magic. I thought that we were special because they came to us. I thought that…that I was special. Now I know that I'm *not*. Just a carp, not a koi…" Bess said through a storm of tears.

Everyone looked at Bess and then each other. Each girl felt the same sort of loss: the loss of being special. Maybe not as strongly as Bess did, but it was there all the same.

Justine was struggling to think of something to help, some words that might make Bess feel better, words to help them *all* feel better. Then, suddenly, she thought of her fish fairy tale.

"Listen, Bess," Justine said, "I still think the koi were magical!"

"You do?" Bess said, looking up at Justine desperately and hoping she was right.

"Before I found my koi, we were all strangers, being picked on every day. Now we are friends and we even made friends with all the little kids and the people at the library and even in the town," Justine continued. "Now that seems magical to me," she said with a smile.

"But that makes the *fish* special. It doesn't make *me* special," Bess sighed sadly.

"I don't think the fish *could* make you special. I think you always *were* special, you just didn't know it! It's like the girl in the story, Bess. She figured out that nothing on the outside could make her happy. It has to come from inside you. Well, I think the same goes for being special. Nothing on the outside, even magical fish, can make you special. You have to be special from the start!" Justine said more confidently. "I think the fish made you *notice* that you are!"

Bess's face wore a frown of concentration, trying to understand what Justine said. "I was special from the start," she repeated, a smile beginning to grow.

"Nobody can take that away from you unless you let them," Justine said.

"Like when they called me Pudgy?" Bess asked.

"Or called me Metal Mouth..." said Alice.

"Or called me Weird Wacko!" chimed in Jan.

"Or called me Dog Bone..." finished Justine.

Everyone began to laugh. It seemed like so long ago that those names stung them with embarrassment, but now they fell away like fall leaves to be crunched underfoot.

"What if they start it up again, when we go back?" Bess asked nervously.

"We give them a withering look, shrug it off, and do the things that make us happy," said Jan boldly.

"But what about Roxy?" asked Bess.

"Just because she couldn't get here, doesn't mean she left us. Have a little faith in her," said Alice.

"And even if she did leave," said Jan, "you still have us!"

"Koi Girls forever!" cried Alice.

CHAPTER SEVENTEEN

Balance is Beautiful

*R*oxy's dad still had a few vacation days left. When he heard Roxy's whole story about the koi, the Koi Girls, everything they had done, everything she had learned this summer, he sat back amazed. She had grown up so much from the sweet, but self-centered little girl he had always known and loved into a sensitive, caring young girl, and it made him feel very proud.

Together they found out what exactly happened at the pond and visited the fish and game commission center where the koi were being held in a tank.

When Roxy approached, the koi immediately came to her. The commissioner was amazed that they had no fear of her and then he understood when he learned that they knew her already.

"They're smart fish all right and can live for a very long time," the commissioner told them.

"How do you think they got into the pond?" asked Roxy's dad.

"Oh, someone probably had small koi in a fish tank and when they got tired of them, they dumped them in the pond," the commissioner said knowingly.

"What will happen to them now? Will they put them back when they're done?" asked Roxy.

"Well, they do disturb the balance of the pond, but if a few changes were made and someone volunteered to care for them, perhaps they could," the commissioner said uncertainly.

That was enough for Roxy. She, with her dad's help, would find a way!

After visiting the Aqua Garden Center, Roxy learned a lot about the care of koi and what was necessary to prepare the pond to receive the carp without destroying the balance of the pond.

At suppertime, her family gathered around the computer to discover more information and prepare to pitch their idea to the town council. Roxy's mom came across something else, a beautiful surprise that would let everyone in the town enjoy the lovely, graceful koi in a way no one had before!

The next day she and her dad met with the town officials and presented their idea. Roxy's dad was able to donate many of the materials necessary and, with the aid of the people at the Aqua Garden Center; they were able to put their plans in place.

That night, Roxy lay in her bed mentally reviewing everything she had learned. She marveled at the beauty of nature and how it delicately worked together. The love of it blossomed in her heart the way nothing ever had before. Suddenly, she knew! This was what made her happy, like writing for Justine, photography for Alice, drawing for Bess, sewing for Jan. This was *her* happiness! She had found it! Oh, baking was fun, but this was different!

She never knew she could be so happy! And she didn't know what made her happier, learning about how nature worked or finding her...what had Jan called it...bliss! That was it! She had found her bliss, and she would follow it! She could not wait to share everything with her friends.

On the next day, she called Justine and asked if she and the girls would meet her at her house because she had a lot to show and tell them. Justine breathed a sigh of relief. Since Bess had brought up the idea of Roxy leaving, it had been spooking her as well. Justine spread the word and before long, they arrived at Roxy's beautiful home.

Roxy couldn't wait to share everything with her friends, and they were overjoyed to hear all her news. They made plans to visit the koi and could not wait for the day when they would be returned to the park.

When that day finally arrived, the mayor announced a grand opening of the new koi pond. Beautiful meditation music filled the air. A group from the tai chi and yoga school put on demonstrations. Many people came to admire the improvements made. They also thanked Roxy's family, and especially Roxy herself, for helping to add this wonderful new addition to the park.

There were park benches placed beside the pond. The weeping willow was still there. The pond ducks still floated about. But there were more water lilies so the fish could hide. And there was something brand new and amazing.

"What is that clear, plastic thing on the water?" asked Jan.

"Just watch," Roxy said with a smile.

Floating like a huge bubble atop the water was a clear plastic dome. It was filled with water. After a moment or two an amazing thing happened. Justine's golden koi appeared in the dome and seemed to float in the air above the water! It waved its fins in a gentle and flowing ballet and then it glided back down below the waterline. One by one, each of the koi appeared in all their glory. It was so breathtaking, the girls could hardly speak!

"That is so amazing!" Jan said finally, breaking the trance they had fallen into.

"We thought so," said Roxy smiling from ear to ear. "It's called a Koi Pearl. My mom came across it on the Internet while we were looking up information on the koi and she thought it was so wonderful that our pond should have one.

"Well, look who is the famous girl now!" said a voice from behind them. The girls turned around to see Samantha, Caroline, and two new girls standing like stunning models.

"Hello, Sam," Roxy said. The Cruel Girls saw that Roxy looked as attractive as ever but she also had an aura of confidence around her that seemed new. Roxy had always been a go-along type, never saying no, doing what the others did without an opinion of her own.

"The pond actually looks nicer now, instead of the sewer it used to be," said Sam, tossing her shiny, gorgeous, long blond hair over her shoulder.

"It was never a *sewer*," mumbled Jan to Alice, who nodded in agreement.

"We thought you'd like to go into the city and school shop," Samantha said, giving the Koi Girls mocking looks.

Bess held her breath, wondering what Roxy would do now that the Cruel Girls were back in town.

"Thanks, but I am going to hang with my friends here," Roxy said lightly and nodding her head toward Justine and the girls.

"You'd rather hang with these freaks?" Samantha said, laughing.

"No, not freaks, *friends*," Roxy said, her hands on her hips, drawing power from her new understanding of herself and what it means to be a friend.

"*Whatever,* suit yourself," said Samantha with a shrug of her shoulders and roll of her eyes. "Just don't come crying to me when you end up with fleas," she taunted as she turned away. "Come on, girls, let's go." The new girls tossed their hair and twittered with laughter.

Samantha started to walk away. The new girls were right on her heels with Caroline in the rear. Samantha carelessly tossed a paper cup she had been holding toward a trashcan but it missed, and she did not stop to pick it up. The other girls walked right by as if it was no big deal to litter.

Roxy was smiling and receiving congratulations from the Koi Girls and they were too busy to notice that Caroline had stopped, considered for a moment, bent down to pick up the cup and placed it in the trash. Then she walked toward Roxy and the girls and said hi. The others stared at her in surprise.

"I really love the changes they made in the pond...Do you guys ever do tai chi? I always wanted to learn...It looks so cool...especially by the pond with the koi and all..."

The Koi Girls did not know what to say. But Roxy realized that Caroline had taken her first step away from the Cruel Girls, or at least she hoped it was.

"No, but you're right! Maybe we can all take some lessons and join the group," Roxy said cheerfully, looking at her friends for support and hopefully agreement.

"Ummm, yeah, it did look cool. I think I would try it," Justine said uncertainly, trying to follow Roxy's lead.

"How did you find out that there were koi in the pond?" she asked.

"Well, it was Justine who saw hers first," Alice said bravely, trying to jump in.

"Which one was that?" said Caroline looking back toward the pond.

"Oh, the gold one, that's Justine's!" said Bess, catching on to what was happening.

"Which one is yours, Jan?" Caroline said.

"Uh, well, the calico one, of course!" Jan said with a laugh and twirled so that her multicolored skirt swirled around her. Everyone laughed with her.

"Where are you guys going now?" asked Caroline.

"Aren't you going shopping with the others?" Roxy asked, taking a chance to see if she was right about Caroline.

"Nah, that stuff...doesn't interest me anymore," she said slowly, deliberately, but looking at her cute, red sandals.

"Do you think I could, you know, hang with you?" she continued and finally looked up to see their reaction.

All the girls looked at each other and none of them seemed to mind.

"Sure," said Justine. "Why not?"

"Look, I'm sorry about how I was...before, you know...I don't want to be that way anymore..." Caroline said, not sure of how to say what she meant.

"People change," Alice said wisely.

"Especially when you are following your bliss," Roxy said with a laugh.

"Your what?" Caroline asked.

Everyone laughed. "We'll explain it to you later; it's a long story!" said Jan.

"Hey, there's the tai chi teacher," said Bess. "Should we try to catch her?"

"Yeah, let's go!" said Justine, as she started to sprint away from the pond and toward the park.

They all scampered off, laughing as they went.

In the pond, in the lovely koi dome, a small red, white, and black koi appeared waving its fins at the fleeing girls.

Printed in Great Britain
by Amazon.co.uk, Ltd.,
Marston Gate.